When Water Makes Mud

A Story of Refugee Children

This story is dedicated to the 200,000 children in the
Bidibidi Refugee Settlement in Uganda who fled from their homes to escape war.

by JANIE REINART   art by MORGAN TAYLOR

BLUE WHALE PRESS
An Imprint of Clear Fork Publishing

Indian Valley Public Library
100 E. Church Ave.
Telford, PA 18969-1720

I make *something* from *nothing* for her.

A *grin skims* across my little sister's face like a *butterfly*. Then . . .

I make *something* from *nothing* for her.

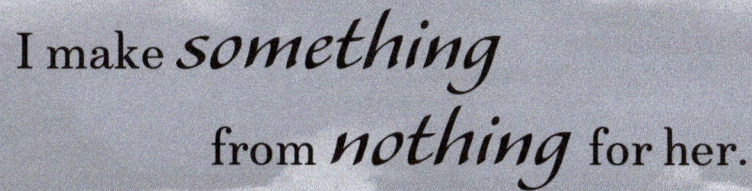

A pebble is a pebble until...

A *smile* *perches*

on my little sister's lips

like a *pigeon*.

Then . . .

I make *something* from *nothing* for her.

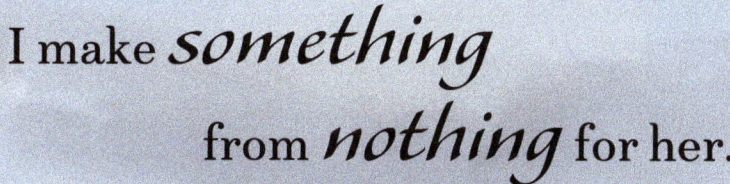

A bag is a bag until . . .

Our *balloon billows* on a *breeze*.

A *giggle bobs* from my little sister's mouth like a *chicken*.

Then . . .

I make *something* from *nothing* for her.

Cardboard is cardboard until . . .

It is gone.

I make *something* from *nothing* for her.

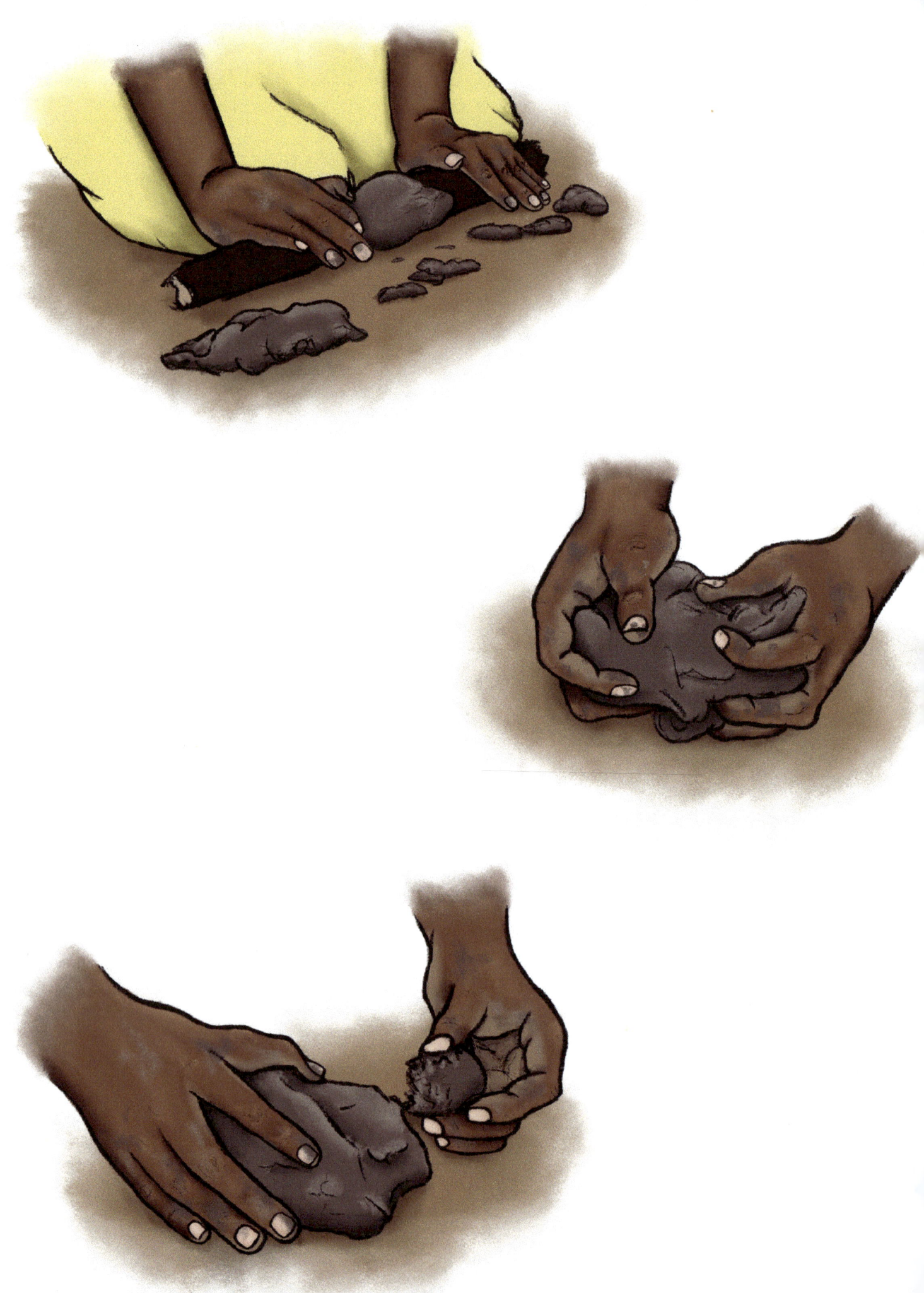

A *laugh leaps* from my little sister's throat like a *goat.*

She *sings* and *sways* her *mud baby.*

In a hundred happy hops *we dance.*

We make something

together

for *tomorrow* . . .

and *dream*. . . .

Susan James, age 10

Photograph by Nora Lorek, which first appeared in *See the Ingenious Toys Made by Refugee Children*, printed online by National Geographic, December 2018, and provided courtesy of Panos Pictures.

AUTHOR'S NOTE

All children love to play. But what if you didn't have any toys? This story is dedicated to the 200,000 children in the Bidibidi Refugee Settlement in Uganda who fled from their homes to escape war. Most arrived with only the clothes they were wearing. The families use some of the animals mentioned in the story—pigeons, chickens, goats—for food, eggs, and milk. The children make handmade toys from found items like mud to sculpt a doll, cardboard to build a car, or a plastic bag with a string to craft a balloon. The youngsters even try to catch and play with grasshoppers. The children use their imaginations to create toys and dream of someday returning home.

—Janie

To all children—keep creating.
—JR

For Cousin Kristin and Aunt Connie. Thank you for encouraging me to keep following my dreams.
—MT

The author wishes to acknowledge and thank photographer Nora Lorek and writer Nina Strochlic whose coverage of children in Uganda inspired this story.

When Water Makes Mud - A Story of Refugee Children

Text copyright © 2021 by Janie Reinart
Illustrations copyright © 2021 by Morgan Taylor
All rights reserved

Picture of Susan is copyright © 2018 Nora Lorek/Panos Pictures and used under license

Published by Blue Whale Press, an imprint of Clear Fork Publishing

No part of this book may be reproduced or transmitted by any means, either mechanical or electronic, or stored in a retrieval system, or otherwise copied for public or private use without obtaining prior permission from the publisher in writing except as allowed under "fair use", which permits quotations embodied in critical articles or reviews.

Contact us at www.clearforkpublishing.com

Address all inquiries to:
Clear Fork Publishing, 102 South Swenson St., Stamford, TX 79553

Publisher's Cataloging-in-Publication data available upon request

Library of Congress Control Number: 2021930465

ISBN: 978-1-950169-43-6 (hardcover)
ISBN: 978-1-950169-44-3 (paperback)

First Edition

With her words, Janie Reinart makes something from nothing. From paper and pencil to page turns, she crafts stories celebrating the creativity and playfulness of children. Janie encourages readers to use their imagination, find their voice, share their stories, and believe in their dreams. She lives in Ohio with her darling husband and delights in playing with her 16 grandchildren. To learn more about Janie, visit janiereinart.com.

Morgan Taylor is a Philadelphia-area native who graduated from Arcadia University's Bachelor of Arts Program for Illustration. She enjoys working mainly in oil paint and digital mediums. Morgan's main focus is portraiture, nature, and things from everyday life. Morgan draws upon various life influences for her work. One of the earliest being her mother's wide use of color in quilting. Additionally, her father would take her to book stores weekly as a child, and she would pick books based on their illustrations. Today, she can often be found either curled up with a good book and a cat or caring for her succulents and cacti. Her goal is to interpret and tell stories through art, and to promote an interest in what makes the seemingly ordinary beautiful. Morgan currently resides in eastern Pennsylvania. You can learn more about her by going to MATillustration.weebly.com.

The publisher's profits from the sale of this book are being donated to UNICEF. You too can help children throughout the world by visiting UNICEF.org.

CPSIA information can be obtained
at www.ICGtesting.com
Printed in the USA
BVHW021259230322
632272BV00002B/4